THE BUK BUK BUK FESTIVAL

Mary Jane and Herm Auch

Holiday House / New York

To Jack Giovanni Auch,
the little boy in the red shirt
and our family's youngest Buk Buk Buk fan . . .
(He loves both books and chickens!)
. . . with love from Nana and Bompa

Text copyright © 2015 by Mary Jane Auch
Illustrations copyright © 2015 by Mary Jane Auch and Herm Auch
All Rights Reserved
HOLIDAY HOUSE is registered in the U.S. Patent and Trademark Office.
Printed and Bound in October 2014 at Toppan Leefung, DongGuan City, China.
www.holidayhouse.com
First Edition
1 3 5 7 9 10 8 6 4 2

Library of Congress Cataloging-in-Publication Data
Auch, Mary Jane.
The buk buk buk festival / by Mary Jane and Herm Auch. — First edition.
pages cm
Summary: Henrietta is a reader and a writer, unusual traits for a chicken, but when
her book is published and she is invited to the Children's Book Festival, only the local
librarian believes she is the author.
ISBN 978-0-8234-3201-1 (hardcover)
[1. Authorship—Fiction. 2. Books and reading—Fiction. 3. Chickens—Fiction.
4. Humorous stories.] I. Auch, Herm, illustrator. II. Title.
PZ7.A898Buk 2015
[E]—dc23
2014017137

Henrietta was an avid reader—a rare talent for a chicken. The librarian let her chick out books because she was eggs-ceedingly careful with them, especially when crossing the road.

Henrietta was also an author. She once wrote her own story and sent it to a publisher, but got a rejection. So she made a few books to give to her aunties and the librarian.

THE PERILS OF MAXINE

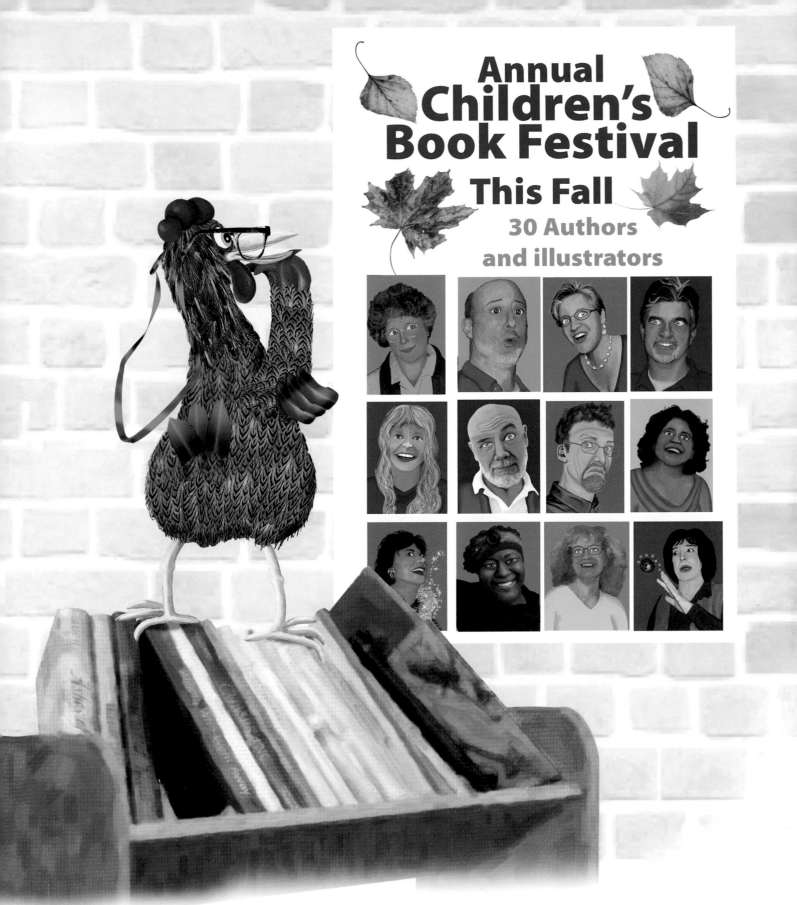

One day Henrietta saw a poster for the Children's Book Festival. She noticed that none of the authors were chickens. "I'll write a new story," she clucked. "This time I'll pretend I'm a person."

Tickety-click. Henrietta pecked out, "Once there was a hen named Chelsea."

"She's writing a new book!" Aunt Liz squawked. The other aunties rushed over.

"Chelsea went walking in the woods," Henrietta typed.

"The old walking-in-the-woods routine?" Aunt Golda yawned. "Hum-drumsticks!"

"Let's play What If," suggested Aunt Olive. "What if Chelsea flies to the moon?"

"I want my story to be about things that chickens really do," Henrietta said.

"All we do is stay cooped up," cackled Aunt Golda.

"Cooped up is cozy," murmured Aunt Zoe.

Henrietta hatched an idea about her coziest memory. "Chelsea felt comfy inside her shell. It fit her perfectly." Henrietta kept going. The story started happy, then got not-so-happy when Chelsea had to leave her shell, and not-happy-at-all when it was time to go to chickergarten.

Hunt & Peck

"That's all right," Henrietta decided. "The main character needs to have a problem to make a good story."

Henrietta cried through the sad parts, then wrote a happy ending.

She sent her story to five publishers with this letter.

Dear Publisher,
I am an expert in chicken behavior. This story comes from observing my own little flock. The name of the story is CHICKERGARTEN.
I hope you enjoy it.
Yours truly,
Henrietta Fowler

Henrietta Fowler seemed like a splendid name for a chicken pretending to be a person.

All five publishers wanted Henrietta's book. She picked the one called Holiday House because they sounded like friendly people who wouldn't get mad if they discovered that she was a chicken after they published her book.

Many months later, a box of books arrived. It took all the hens to push it and pullet into the coop. Henrietta's aunties made her read *Chickergarten* aloud over and over. "I remember how you loved your little shell," sighed Aunt Zoe.

Books
Handle
With Care

To
Henrietta
wler
enway Dr.
io

Later that day, Henrietta took her new book to the library.

"We already have *Chickergarten*," said the librarian. "It got a starred review in *The Corn Book*."

Henrietta read the review to her aunties. They weren't impressed. Aunt Golda thought the star was a bug and ate it.

The next day, Henrietta was flabbergasted to see *Chickergarten* in the bookstore. When she got home, she had the most egg-citing surprise of all.

Dear Henrietta Fowler,
We love your book,
Chickergarten. We
cordially invite you to
be a featured author
in our Children's Book
Festival.

Henrietta didn't need to
brood over the invitation.
She eggs-cepted right away.

Book Festival

ew this Year Henrietta Fowler

The day of the Children's Book Festival,
Henrietta joined the crowds headed for the door.
Inside, authors sat at tables with stacks of their
books. Up near the ceiling, their names were spelled
out in moving lights. Henrietta's feathers fluttered
when she saw her own name.

Then she spotted her books and flew up to her table. "This is the proudest moment of my eggs-istence," she clucked to the author next to her.

"Eeeeek!" screamed the author. Henrietta looked up, expecting to see a hawk, but there was none in sight.

"Aaaaaak!" yelled the author behind her. Henrietta looked down the aisle, thinking a fox had sneaked in . . . but no.

The festival director came running. "Who let this chicken in here?"

"I'm an author!" Henrietta squawked. But even though she knew people language, Henrietta's words came out in henspeak. Nobody could understand her . . .

Henrietta Fow...
AUTH...

... so she ran ...

. . . and ran, then dived under a table.
Henrietta huddled, crestfallen, in the darkness
until a child discovered her hiding place.

Then she escaped to perch high on a balloon, where she could see the whole festival. In a corner down below, a woman was tapping on a computer. She was the one making the words in moving lights! When the woman left the table, Henrietta swooped down.

Chicken loose in the hall

THERE IS A CHICKEN LOOSE IN HALL ...

She pecked out a frantic bulletin.

I MAY BE A CHICKEN BUT I'M ALSO AN AUTHOR. MY NAME IS HENRIETTA FOWLER AND I WROTE CHICKERGARTEN

Way across the room, the librarian saw the message. "Henrietta! Where are you?" she shouted.

"Buk buk buk BUK!" Henrietta screeched. The librarian came running, picking up Henrietta just in time.

"Get that chicken out of here!" yelled the festival director.

Henrietta Fowler
AUTHOR

The librarian held the frightened hen in her arms. "This is Henrietta Fowler, the author of *Chickergarten*."

"Ridiculous!" said the director. "Chickens can't write."

The loyal librarian smiled. "That's what makes Henrietta unique. A chicken who can write books is a national treasure."

For the rest of the day, the librarian opened the books for Henrietta to scratch her autograph in every one. Henrietta was enchanted to meet her fans.

CHICKERGARTEN

CHICKERGARTEN

BY
Henrietta
Fowler

And she felt eggs-traordinarily proud to be a chicken.

Big Eggs-citement at the Children's Book Festival

The usually peaceful Children's Book Festival was a chaotic scene yesterday when a live chicken flapped through the exhibit hall pursued by festival organizers.

The day was also marred by the absence of the Featured New Author, Henrietta Fowler. Her picture book, CHICKERGARTEN, follows the early life of a chick.

"Fowler's absence is a huge disappointment," said Festival Director Myrna Flooz. "CHICKERGARTEN is the most popular book with area children. They have been so excited to meet her."

"I wanted to ask her how she thinks like a chicken," said 8-year-old Brian Glass. "Now I'll never know."

The mysteries of the runaway chicken and the absent author were solved simultaneously when it was revealed that Henrietta Fowler is a chicken!

"A chicken who can write a book! How cool is that?" said Glass as he waited in a long line to have Fowler autograph his book.